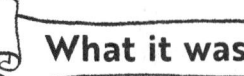

What it was like

ANCIENT EGYPTIAN

DAVID LONG

Illustrated by
Stefano Tambellini

Barrington Stoke

This book was written under some duress and is gratefully dedicated to Mr Nitin Gupta and his team at West Suffolk Hospital.

Published by Barrington Stoke
An imprint of HarperCollins*Publishers*
Westerhill Road, Bishopbriggs, Glasgow, G64 2QT

www.barringtonstoke.co.uk

HarperCollins*Publishers*
Macken House, 39/40 Mayor Street Upper,
Dublin 1, DO1 C9W8, Ireland

First published in 2025

Text © 2025 David Long
Illustrations © 2025 Stefano Tambellini
Cover design © 2025 HarperCollins*Publishers* Limited

The moral right of David Long and Stefano Tambellini to be identified as the author and illustrator of this work has been asserted in accordance with the Copyright, Designs and Patents Act, 1988

ISBN 978-0-00-870053-9

10 9 8 7 6 5 4 3 2 1

All rights reserved. No part of this publication may be reproduced, stored in a retrieval system, or transmitted, in whole or in any part in any form or by any means, electronic, mechanical, photocopying, recording or otherwise without the prior permission in writing of the publisher and copyright owners

The contents of this publication are believed correct at the time of printing. Nevertheless the publisher can accept no responsibility for errors or omissions, changes in the detail given or for any expense or loss thereby caused

A catalogue record for this book is available from the British Library

Printed and bound in India by Replika Press Pvt. Ltd.

This book contains FSC™ certified paper and other controlled sources to ensure responsible forest management.

For more information visit: www.harpercollins.co.uk/green

CONTENTS

1. **POWER AND PYRAMIDS**   1
   Who Were the Ancient Egyptians?

2. **SURVIVING UNDER A SCORCHING SUN**   7
   The River and the Desert

3. **THE RULERS AND THE RULED**   19
   The Pharaohs and Their Queens

4. **AN EMPIRE BUILT ON FOOD**   31
   Life on the Land

5. **BUILDING A GREAT CIVILISATION**   43
   Architects, Engineers and Artists

6. **SYMBOLS AND CYMBALS**   56
   Religion, Writing and Music

7. **THE AFTERLIFE**   68
   Mummies and Grave Robbers

8. **WONDERFUL THINGS**   79
   Tutankhamun and His Treasure

9. **THE END OF THE EMPIRE**   89
   Egypt Today

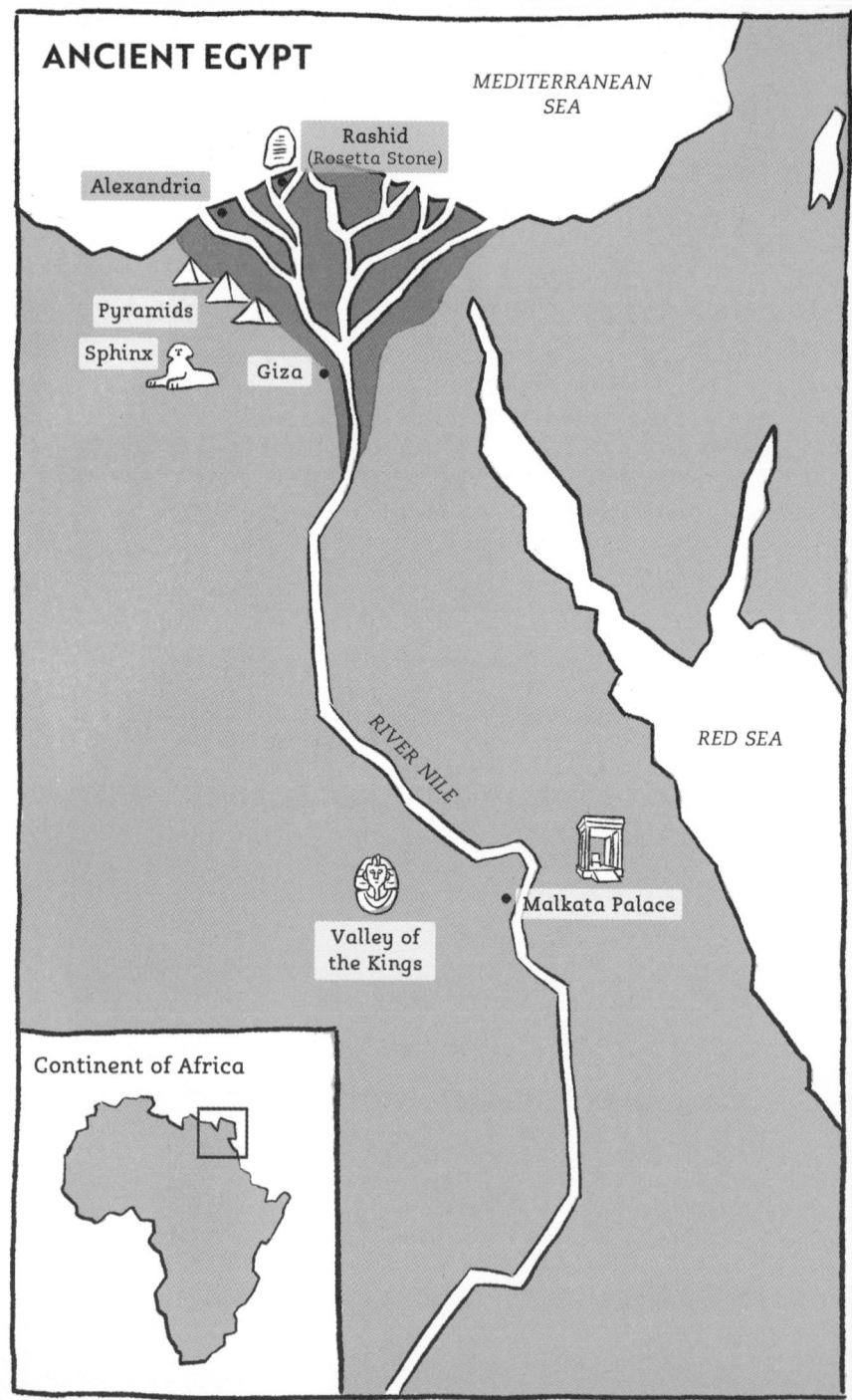

1
POWER AND PYRAMIDS

Who Were the Ancient Egyptians?

The people we call the ancient Egyptians began farming in an area of north-east Africa more than 7,000 years ago. Their land wasn't known as Egypt then but Kemet. It was mostly dry desert, so the farmers and their families chose to live close to the River Nile.

The Nile is the longest river in the world and made it possible for people to survive in this harsh environment. The Egyptians' farming skills and profits from trading with neighbouring countries meant they built a rich and powerful civilisation. This was ruled by pharaohs, and it lasted for around 3,000 years.

During the pharaohs' reign, Egyptians built the largest buildings the world had ever seen. The most famous of these are the pyramids, which were built as tombs for royalty. More than 130 pyramids are still standing, and they attract millions of visitors every year.

The pyramids show that the Egyptians were highly organised and far more advanced than any country in Europe at the time. As well as these spectacular buildings, they created a way of writing (using simple pictures called hieroglyphics) and were very good at mathematics.

They wrote on a type of paper called papyrus, which was made from the reeds growing along the Nile. This was lighter and much easier to use than the clay tablets people had written on before.

POWER AND PYRAMIDS

The Egyptians we know the most about were the pharaohs. When they died, their bodies were carefully preserved before they were buried using a process called mummification. Many of these mummies are on display in modern museums and are popular exhibits.

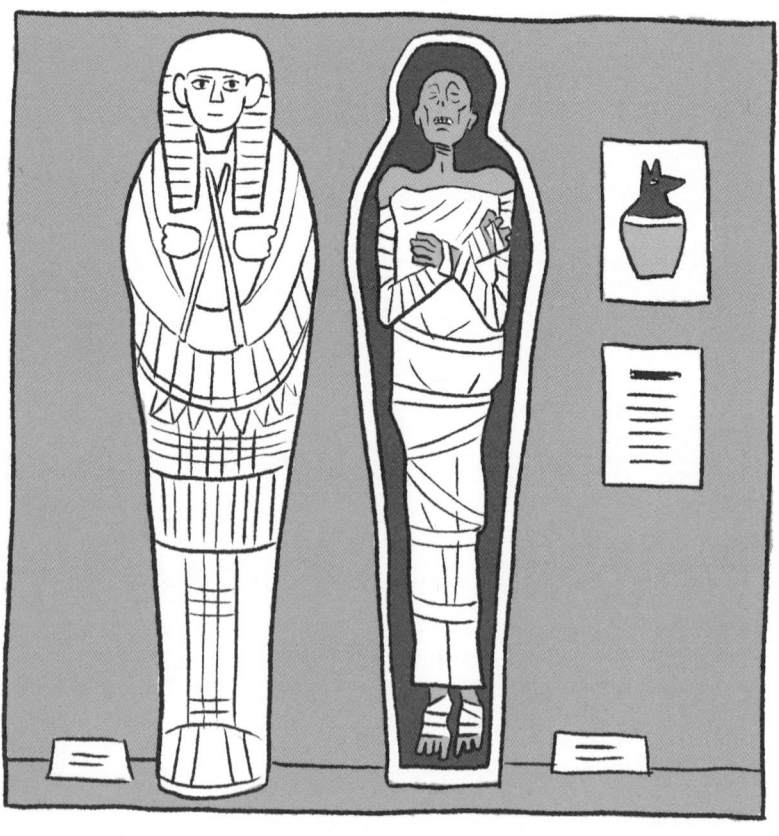

We also know a lot about how ordinary Egyptian families lived. They worshipped hundreds of different gods, and most Egyptians enjoyed music and dancing. They liked wearing wigs, and red, green and black make-up (including the men). Everyone who could afford to wore perfume and elaborate pieces of jewellery.

The ancient Egyptians were also highly inventive. They were the first to make ploughs pulled by animals instead of humans, and the first to use special curved blades for harvesting their crops. They came up with a solar calendar to measure the seasons using the sun, and used at least two different types of clocks for telling the time.

The first ever toothpaste was also an Egyptian invention. This was made by mixing together salt, pepper, mint and dried flowers. It must have tasted very strange, and no one makes toothpaste this way now, but a lot of other modern inventions are based on ancient Egyptian ideas.

The Egyptians' empire collapsed over 2,000 years ago, but it is impossible not to admire the energy, cleverness and imagination of these people.

2
SURVIVING UNDER A SCORCHING SUN

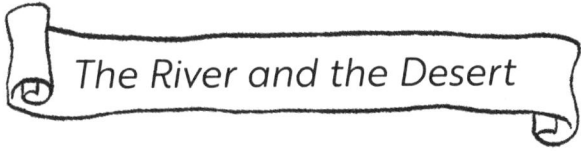

The River and the Desert

The huge desert surrounding Egypt's towns and cities was seemingly endless, but also vital as it protected them. An invading army would have to march across thousands of kilometres of rock and sand without dying of thirst or hunger. However, the empire could not have existed without the enormous River Nile winding across the landscape. Its waters helped to transform a very dry, harsh place into an area where millions of people could grow food and survive.

SURVIVING UNDER A SCORCHING SUN

The Nile stretches more than 6,500 kilometres from end to end, which is almost as far as the distance between England and India. As well as supplying the water Egyptians needed to live, the river provided jobs for hundreds of thousands of people who worked on the river or its banks. The largest group of these were the farmers who used the water to raise the crops and animals needed to feed a population of more than two million people.

This was possible because every year the Nile flooded a large area of the desert, and the floods left behind huge amounts of rich, dark-coloured mud. The thick, sticky mud improved the sandy soil in the farmers' fields. It was useful in other ways too. Egyptian builders used it to construct the simple flat-roofed houses that most families lived in.

The mud was formed into neat brick shapes when it was still wet and then left in the sun to bake hard. Once a house was finished, its walls

were painted white to reflect the sun's heat. This helped keep the inside of the house cool during the summer, but when it got really hot, families often slept up on the roof.

Houses built using mud were much cheaper than stone ones, but the brickmakers had to be very careful when gathering the mud from the river. The marshy banks of the Nile were home to many dangerous animals, such as hippos and crocodiles, deadly scorpions and poisonous snakes called cobras. Surprisingly, this didn't stop many young Egyptians from enjoying a swim in the river or play-fighting pretend battles as they floated on small homemade rafts.

There were many less dangerous animals in the Nile too. These included lots of different fish, and most of them were good to eat. Egyptians learned to catch these fish using nets, traps and a sharp spear called a harpoon. They usually did this standing on the riverbank or in a small boat constructed from reeds tied into fat bundles.

Fish such as perch, tilapia, mullet, carp and eels were an important part of almost every Egyptian's diet. They could be roasted, boiled or fried, or dried and covered in salt, which preserved them for several months.

The Nile was also the main transport route in ancient Egypt, so it was often crowded with boatmen, sailors, merchants and traders.

SURVIVING UNDER A SCORCHING SUN

There were no proper roads on land, so boats of all sizes travelled up and down the Nile, carrying cargo as well as passengers. Even the pharaohs travelled on the river, usually on large and luxurious royal barges.

The Egyptians were expert sailors, and over time they moved from using little boats and rafts made of reed bundles to ships and boats constructed of wood. Some of these were so large they could carry enormous loads of the heavy stones used for building temples, pyramids and other impressive buildings. Smaller boats were used to transport animals, food and pottery jars containing wine and olive oil.

The wooden planks used to construct these boats were held together using knotted rope because even the best boat builders didn't know how to make metal screws or nails. The rope was made by twisting reeds or palm-tree leaves.

The Nile flowed from the south to the north, but the wind usually blew in the opposite direction. The sailors worked out that they could raise a sail to travel in one direction using wind power and then rely on the river's current to take their boats the other way when it was time to return home.

Current flowing to the north

This was much easier than rowing long distances and meant that boat owners didn't need to employ many strong oarsmen to power their vessels. The boats still had oars, but they were only needed to steer. Having a small crew on even a large ship made river transport fairly cheap. This meant that merchants who

Wind blowing to the south

traded with other countries were able to make even larger profits for the wealthy Egyptian empire.

Even when the Nile wasn't flooding, it was used by farmers to water the crops in their fields. They dug hundreds of small canals and ditches along the riverbanks. The canals were much narrower than the Nile, but when the river wasn't flooding, they allowed the water to flow out of the river and into the surrounding countryside.

Farmers used an invention called a *shaduf*, which is a cross between a hand-powered crane and a large bucket. These lifted water out of the ditches and poured it onto their fields.

This made it possible to grow crops that would otherwise have been killed by the heat and dry soil, such as wheat, onions, leeks, garlic and beans.

SURVIVING UNDER A SCORCHING SUN

Wheat was important because it could be traded with countries where the farmers were less productive or couldn't grow their own wheat because of the climate. Normally, it was exchanged for things the Egyptians didn't have themselves. This included thousands of trees every year. The wood was needed to build ships because large trees were rare in Egypt. Wheat was also traded for valuable gemstones, spices and elephant ivory, and for useful metals such as copper, iron and tin.

PHARAOH

VIZIERS & PRIESTS

SCRIBES & SOLDIERS

CRAFTSMEN, ARTISTS & MERCHANTS

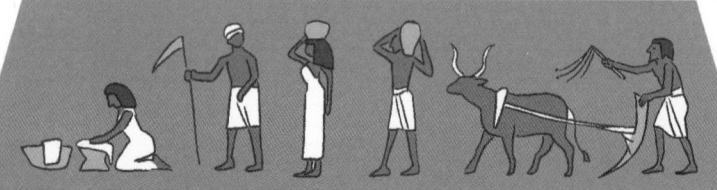

FARMERS & ENSLAVED PEOPLE

3

THE RULERS AND THE RULED

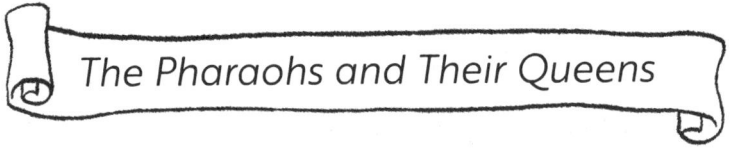

The Pharaohs and Their Queens

The difference between rich and poor people in ancient Egypt was enormous. However, even the lives of ordinary families were better than in many other parts of the world.

Most Egyptians had their own homes, although only the very rich had things like an indoor loo and comfortable furniture. People had jobs, including many women, and this meant they could afford to feed their families and enjoy themselves on their days off.

The very poorest were the many thousands of enslaved people. They were given food, shelter and clothing, and didn't have to pay taxes like other Egyptians, but in times of famine they were probably the first people to starve.

The lifestyle of the pharaohs and their families was very different to this. They were not just the richest Egyptians but also some of the richest people who have ever lived. A pharaoh usually inherited the kingdom from his father.

Unlike ordinary Egyptians, pharaohs were allowed to have as many wives as they liked. One pharaoh, Ramses II, married so many times that it is believed he had more than a hundred children!

Most pharaohs had a wife who was more important than all of his others. She was known as the Great Royal Wife and was the

THE RULERS AND THE RULED 21

most powerful woman in the empire. Very few women ever became pharaohs themselves.

Some historians think that the pharaoh Akhenaten allowed his wife Nefertiti to rule Egypt alongside him. But usually a woman only ruled Egypt when there were no men in the family to take over the throne after the old pharaoh died.

It could also happen if the pharaoh's favourite son was too young to rule on his own. Then the boy's mother would occupy the throne until he was older. However, one woman who did this refused to give up the throne when her son became an adult. She was called Hatshepsut, and she successfully ruled Egypt for more than 20 years.

Whoever ruled the Egyptian empire enjoyed a life full of wonderful ceremonies, beautiful palaces and incredible luxury. Egyptians believed the pharaoh was divine, which means god-like. The pharaoh owned much of the land in Egypt and ruled by royal decree. This meant that the pharaoh decided what the laws were, and everyone else had to obey them.

The royal family had many different palaces to choose from because pharaohs liked to build new ones when they inherited the throne.

THE RULERS AND THE RULED

One palace, called Malkata, was so large that it took 18 years to build and covered 50 hectares – almost the size of 2,000 tennis courts. Anyone who wanted to see the whole of the outside would have to walk more than 2.8 kilometres around the walls.

These spacious palaces contained royal apartments for the pharaoh and all his children, plus accommodation and offices for the most senior priests and officials. They had large meeting halls and various temples that were arranged around courtyards and gardens. Each queen was given her own separate part of the palace and dozens of her own servants.

Malkata also had a harbour that was linked to the River Nile by a series of man-made canals. These meant the pharaoh could leave the palace on his own ship.

Royal vessels were made of the finest imported wood, and most were covered in rich carvings and colourful painted decorations. The largest ship we know about was built with over 1,000 planks of expensive cedar wood and was more than 40 metres long.

THE RULERS AND THE RULED

Its size meant this ship was very heavy, but it was also slim and elegant. It had to be large because it carried everything that the pharaoh might need on a long journey.

This included special items of furniture called litters. These were a bit like luxurious beds and were made to move the pharaoh from place to place in comfort. Members of the royal family were far too important to walk anywhere, so teams of strong enslaved people had to carry them around in these litters. This happened whenever the pharaoh or his queens wanted to leave the ship or travel anywhere outside one of the palaces.

THE RULERS AND THE RULED

The pharaoh didn't have to wash himself or dress and undress. Egyptians liked to keep clean, but these duties were carried out by special palace servants.

Servants also had to put on the pharaoh's fabulous solid gold and silver jewellery, and looked after his *pschent*, which was a crown.

Egyptians expected the pharaoh to look amazing every time he was seen in public, so great care was taken over his appearance. The royal jewellery was especially eye-catching and used precious stones such as blue lapis lazuli, purple amethyst and dazzling green malachite.

We know that the pharaohs had time to enjoy their hobbies. Many of them raced horse-drawn chariots for fun or hunted wild animals such as ostriches and elephants.

THE RULERS AND THE RULED

But a pharaoh also had a lot of work to do as the ruler of an empire nearly four times larger than the UK. Priests and senior palace officials known as viziers were by his side to advise him, but it was always up to the pharaoh to make the final decisions.

The main tasks of the pharaoh included choosing what laws were needed to ensure order was kept in society and deciding whether or not to go to war against Egypt's enemies. The pharaoh also fixed the level of taxes that people had to pay. These taxes were used to fund Egypt's enormous army and navy, and to build extravagant new temples and other grand buildings.

The pharaoh was also involved in the religious lives of every Egyptian person. One of the greatest pharaohs, Thutmose III, ruled Egypt for more than half a century and ordered the construction of at least 50 new temples. Pharaohs were expected to take a central role in the many religious festivals and ceremonies held in the temples during the year.

The pharaoh's involvement in religion was essential because ancient Egyptians believed that their ruler was an important link between themselves and all of their gods.

Above all else, they wanted the gods to ensure that their lives were fair and harmonious. This was a concept they called *Ma'at*, and part of it required the pharaoh to be fair and reasonable. Most of the pharaohs tried to be, but unpopular pharaohs were sometimes murdered because people didn't like the way they ran the empire.

4
AN EMPIRE BUILT ON FOOD

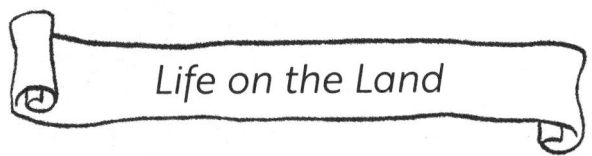
Life on the Land

The most common job in Ancient Egypt was farming. Children as young as four or five helped their parents look after the family's crops and animals.

Everyone worked hard to raise sheep, cows, pigs, goats, ducks and geese, but only the royal family was allowed to keep chickens. Pigeons were sometimes caught and fattened up to eat, and bees were kept to make wax and honey.

Farmwork was exhausting in a hot climate, especially without any machinery and using

AN EMPIRE BUILT ON FOOD

only simple wooden or stone tools. But it was better than many other jobs, such as fighting in the army or digging for valuable metals and gemstones in the mines the pharaoh owned.

Farming the Land

AN EMPIRE BUILT ON FOOD

Ploughing became a lot easier when cattle called oxen were trained to pull ploughs, and tough donkeys were useful if a farmer needed to move any heavy loads.

Collecting water with a shaduf

Ploughing with oxen

Canals dug to bring water

Growing crops

Children helping

Egyptians divided their year into three seasons, not four like we do today. The first season was called *akhet*, which was when the River Nile flooded the fields and fruit orchards.

When this happened, it was impossible to work in them, so farmers and their families looked for temporary jobs in their local towns. Many found employment as builders, sometimes helping with large construction projects such as a new temple or a gigantic pyramid.

These people only returned to their fields at the start of the next season, which was called *peret*. This was when they ploughed the wet, newly enriched soil and planted the seeds needed to grow the crops.

The last season was *shemu*, harvest-time, when the crops were ripe and ready to be cut down. The harvest was stored to feed the farmer's family or taken by donkey to be sold at local markets.

Akhet (flood)
SEPTEMBER – JANUARY

Peret (planting)
JANUARY – MAY

Shemu (harvest)
MAY – SEPTEMBER

Understanding the seasons was essential in a country where the lack of rainfall could lead to droughts and famine. If the Egyptians made a mistake and planted their seeds too early or too late, nothing would grow. Hundreds of thousands of people could starve to death as a result.

Egyptians believed that their gods made the crops grow tall and strong, so part of every harvest was given to the temples to keep the gods happy.

Emmer was one of the most important crops. It's a type of wheat that, along with another grain called barley, was used to make bread and a sweet-tasting beer.

Beer was very popular and part of almost every Egyptian's normal diet. Workers often received it as part of their pay, and even very young children drank beer at home several times a day.

AN EMPIRE BUILT ON FOOD 37

Emmer wheat

Beer jug

Barley grains

The beer was probably safer to drink than dirty river water. Most of the beer brewers were women, who sold it in jugs from street stalls. Their customers usually drank it with a straw in order to avoid swallowing the grains at the bottom of the jug.

Sometimes, beer was flavoured with nuts, herbs or rose petals for special occasions. Rich Egyptians drank beer too, but at banquets they preferred to serve wine, which was an expensive luxury.

Cereals such as wheat and barley were sold abroad in huge amounts to countries in need. For example, the rival Roman Empire, which was centred on Italy, was unable to grow enough wheat to feed its fast-growing population. Romans ate a lot of bread, just like the Egyptians, so Egypt became an important source of the grain they needed to make flour.

Onions and garlic were also very popular in Egypt. The farmers were so good at watering their fields artificially that these crops could grow even when there was hardly any rain. This also meant that crops such as lettuces, cucumbers, grapes, plums, pomegranates and watermelons could grow.

There were many things that Egyptians didn't grow, however. Their farmers had never even heard of crops that are eaten by many people today, such as tomatoes, bananas and potatoes. Despite this, even poor families enjoyed a healthy diet of fruit and vegetables,

AN EMPIRE BUILT ON FOOD

along with any fish they caught in the Nile. However, the rich Egyptians ate most of the meat and eggs.

Everyone ate with their fingers (including the pharaoh), but good table manners were very important. Egyptians ate three meals a day and always washed their hands first. Young children were taught that it was rude to stare at their food and not to leave anything to be thrown away. This was probably because growing crops in the desert needed much hard work and because Egyptians believed their food was a precious gift from the gods.

However, not everything that the Egyptians grew and harvested each shemu was for eating. We've already seen how the lush green papyrus reeds growing down by the Nile could be used to make everything from writing paper to ropes and even sailing boats.

AN EMPIRE BUILT ON FOOD

Reeds were also perfect to weave and make into baskets and for making the sandals that nearly everyone wore. The Egyptians even found uses for the reeds' tough wooden roots, which could be turned into eating bowls or burned as fuel in village bread ovens.

Another important crop not used for food was a plant called flax. This was used to make a type of cloth called linen. Flax is the oldest clothing material we're aware of – the oldest piece ever discovered dates back more than 6,000 years. Linen is very light and cool, so it was worn by almost everyone in Egypt, rich as well as poor.

Not surprisingly, the clothes of the rich were of a higher quality and much more decorative than everyone else's. The pharaoh's clothes were made of the very best linen, which was harvested when the flax reeds were still young and soft. Poorer Egyptians' clothes were more basic, such as simple wraparound white skirts made from very cheap linen that was coarse and scratchy.

Most children didn't wear anything at all until they were six years old. Their hair was often left uncut until the age of three, and after that, little girls usually had pigtails, while their brothers often had shaved heads with a single plait down one side.

5
BUILDING A GREAT CIVILISATION

Architects, Engineers and Artists

Not everyone in ancient Egypt was a farmer. Most children learned about work from their parents and spent their lives doing the same jobs as them. This meant some children were trained from a young age to become artists or craftspeople.

They learned how to paint or to carve wood and stone, or make clothing, jewellery, cooking pots and other everyday items. Others learned how to design buildings, some of which became the largest and most impressive structures in the whole of the ancient world.

BUILDING A GREAT CIVILISATION

The pyramids on the west bank of the River Nile are the best known of these. Other impressive buildings include gigantic statues of mythical creatures as well as gods and pharaohs. These took years or even decades to complete. The fact that so many have survived is one of the reasons people today find the ancient Egyptians so interesting.

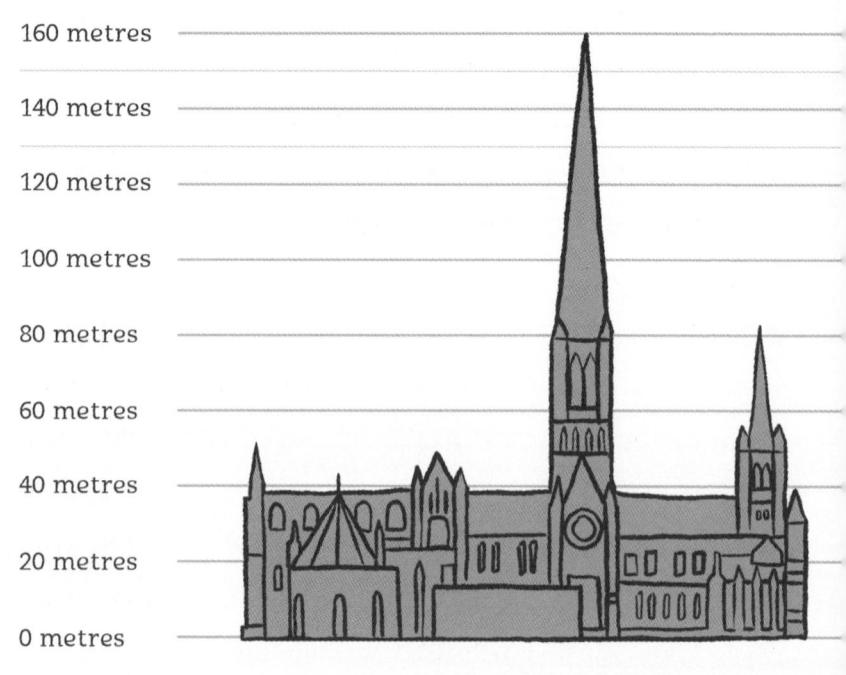

Lincoln Cathedral: 160m

BUILDING A GREAT CIVILISATION

The Great Pyramid of Giza is by far the largest building. It was made as a tomb for Pharaoh Khufu, who ruled Egypt more than 4,500 years ago. It is thought to weigh approximately 5.7 million tonnes, and when it was finished, it was the tallest building in the world at nearly 147 metres. The pyramid held this record for an amazing 3,800 years until it was finally overtaken by Lincoln Cathedral in England in the fourteenth century.

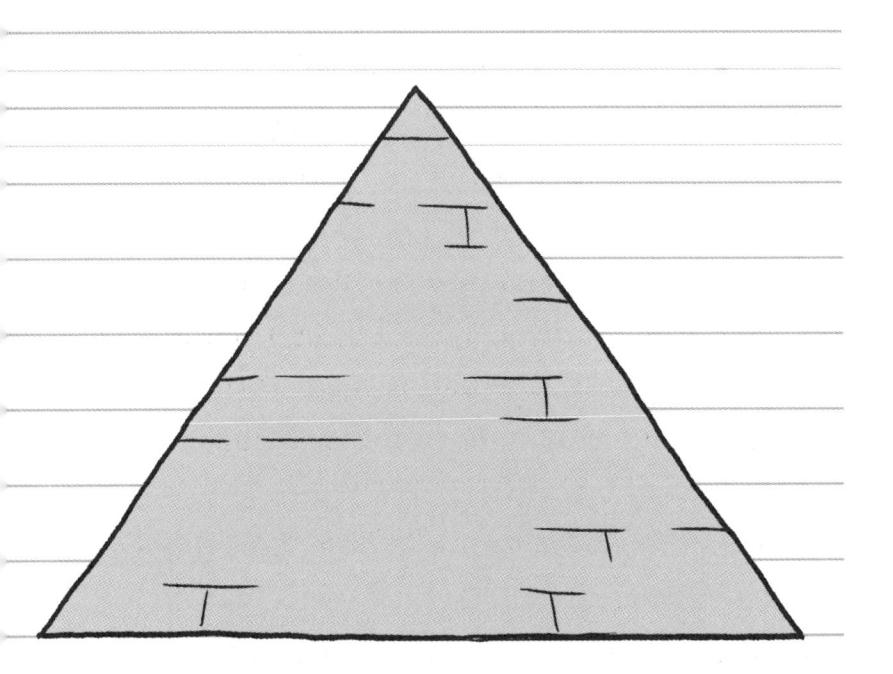

Great Pyramid of Giza: 146.6m

Historians are not sure which architect built the Great Pyramid of Giza. It may have been a priest called Hemiunu who organised a team of 20,000 strong, skilled workers. He was the nephew of Pharaoh Khufu and one of his most important officials.

More than 2.3 million blocks of stone had to be brought from quarries hundreds of kilometres away to create this pyramid. The heaviest blocks weighed up to 80 tonnes and each one had to be cut to the right shape, lifted into place and then fitted together very precisely. This was all done by hand.

Smaller pyramids were built nearby for two of Khufu's wives, Meritites and Henutsen. Today, it is hard to imagine how all these were built without any modern tools or machinery.

Experts who have studied the pyramids closely think the stone blocks were probably dragged across the scorching desert on wooden sledges. They were then pulled up giant earth ramps that Egyptian engineers designed to reach the top of each new pyramid. Rollers made of tree trunks may have helped to move the blocks up the slopes. Even with this, it is thought to have taken more than 20 years to finish Khufu's tomb.

In other parts of the country, Egyptian engineers helped with the construction of the canals along the banks of the Nile and built the world's first lighthouse.

The lighthouse was known as the Pharos of Alexandria and had a huge metal mirror on the top to reflect the sun's rays.

The canals used to water the fields also worked as drains to prevent the annual Nile flood from wrecking people's homes. This is something called hydraulic engineering, and ancient Egypt was one of the first civilisations to understand how it worked. Building these things would have required very precise measurements and careful calculations

BUILDING A GREAT CIVILISATION

to get everything right, and we still don't understand how the Egyptians managed to do this.

How the country's many giant stone pillars were built is just as mysterious. These are known as obelisks and were created using hard, heavy stone that had to be carved by hand. Then somehow they were moved into an upright position using only ropes and human strength. The stonemasons who created them had only simple copper chisels and wooden mallets but were able to carve highly complex designs into the stone. They also created immense statues to decorate the pharaohs' palaces and temples.

The Great Sphinx at Giza is easily the most impressive of the statues we know about. It represents a strange creature with a human head and a lion's body that is more than 70 metres long and 20 metres tall. It is even older than most of the pyramids and is the largest statue in the world.

BUILDING A GREAT CIVILISATION 51

Other impressive examples of the stonemasons' skills include an enormous granite statue of Pharaoh Ramses II, which weighs more than a dozen elephants, and a pair of statues known as the Colossi of Memnon. These are twin sculptures of a pharaoh called Amenhotep III sitting down, and each statue is 18 metres tall.

These statues make the pharaohs seem like giants, but Egypt's artists and craftspeople didn't always work on this massive scale. The walls of many tombs are covered in tiny but highly detailed decorations.

Some small statues of gods and pharaohs are just a few centimetres tall but as beautifully made as Amenhotep's. Most statues, large or small, were originally painted in wonderful bright colours, but over thousands of years the paint has sadly faded or worn away.

Egypt's craftspeople were also experts at designing and making jewellery, produced in many small workshops across the empire. Nearly everyone could afford jewellery of some sort, and everyone, young and old, loved wearing it.

Of course, not everyone could afford jewel-encrusted gold and silver pieces like the pharaoh. Even a string of simple glass beads would have been too expensive for most Egyptians.

So jewellers created colourful rings, earrings, bracelets, anklets and necklaces out of more basic materials. For example, they used wood that had been carved and polished or painted, and cheap clay made of mud from the Nile.

Jewellery was clearly very important to Egyptians whatever the material. The pharaoh sometimes gave away expensive jewels as gifts to his favourite officials and military commanders.

Painted portraits from this time usually show the person wearing his or her favourite jewellery, which is how we know what sorts of styles people liked.

Jewellery was often symbolic for those who owned it – even the most basic examples made out of wood or clay.

Some items known as amulets were believed to have magical powers to bring the wearer good luck or to keep away evil spirits.

Often these featured animal designs that Egyptians thought were lucky. Scarab beetles were popular, as well as cats and even flies.

This symbolism explains why many Egyptians were buried with their jewellery when they died. Archaeologists often find jewellery when they excavate ancient graves.

Their findings can tell them a lot about the person who died, not simply how rich and well dressed they were.

They have also shown how Egyptian tastes and fashions changed over nearly 3,000 years.

6
SYMBOLS AND CYMBALS

Religion, Writing and Music

Ancient Egyptians took great care with burials because their society was very religious. They worshipped so many different gods and goddesses that we don't know all their names or even how many there were. The total number of gods was probably more than 2,000, and they were so important to everyone living in the empire that there were special prayers and spells for almost every aspect of daily life.

Egyptians believed that the gods were always watching what they did and that particular gods were in charge of certain things. Fisherman on the Nile, for example, prayed to a fish goddess called Hatmehit. They hoped that if she heard their prayers, she would help them to catch lots of fish. It was believed the god Osiris controlled the flooding of the River Nile each year to make it possible for Egypt's farmers to grow enough food. Another god called Ptah watched over all the builders and craftspeople.

For a long time, the most important god was Ra (or Re) – the sun god who ruled over the Earth and sky. He also governed the afterlife, which is where Egyptians believed they would go when they died.

Artists usually showed these gods as half-human and half-animal when they made paintings or statues of them. Many had human bodies with the faces of animals, such as Anubis, who had the head of a jackal (a kind of wild dog), and Horus, who had the head of a falcon. Bastet had a woman's body and a cat's face and ears, and for a long time it was believed she was an evil demon. Egyptians didn't think all their gods were good, but over time Bastet changed to become the goddess of pleasure.

HATMEHIT

PTAH

OSIRIS

RA

ANUBIS

BASTET

HORUS

After the pharaoh and his family, priests were among the most important people in ancient Egypt because they were the link to the gods. They were known as the "servants of the gods", but unlike ordinary servants they were often rich and very powerful. Most of the priests were men, but women could also serve as priests in some of the temples.

Priests were in charge of the temples, and they organised religious festivals throughout the year as well as important national events like the crowning of a new pharaoh. However, thousands of other people were involved in the religious life of ancient Egypt, and their work was also important.

The hieroglyphic alphabet invented by the Egyptians was very sophisticated, but most ordinary people never learned how to read or write. Instead, they relied on people called scribes to help them. Scribes read and wrote letters and explained the meaning of official tax or legal documents. Scribes also wrote the contracts when people decided to marry.

The vast majority of scribes were men. Many of them were based in the temples, which meant they had to understand hieratic, which was a special form of writing used by the priests, as well as normal hieroglyphics and mathematics.

For a long time, those who studied ancient Egypt were baffled by the scribes' hieroglyphics. They were very beautiful but seemed like a secret code that no one could read or understand.

It wasn't until the nineteenth century that the code was broken – with the help of a large black rock called the Rosetta Stone.

SYMBOLS AND CYMBALS

The rock had been discovered at the end of the eighteenth century by a group of French soldiers near an Egyptian town called Rashid. The Rosetta Stone had three different forms of writing scratched into its surface, including long lines of complicated hieroglyphics. After studying the writing on the stone for several years, European scholars were finally able to crack the code. It meant that people could read and understand all three languages at last.

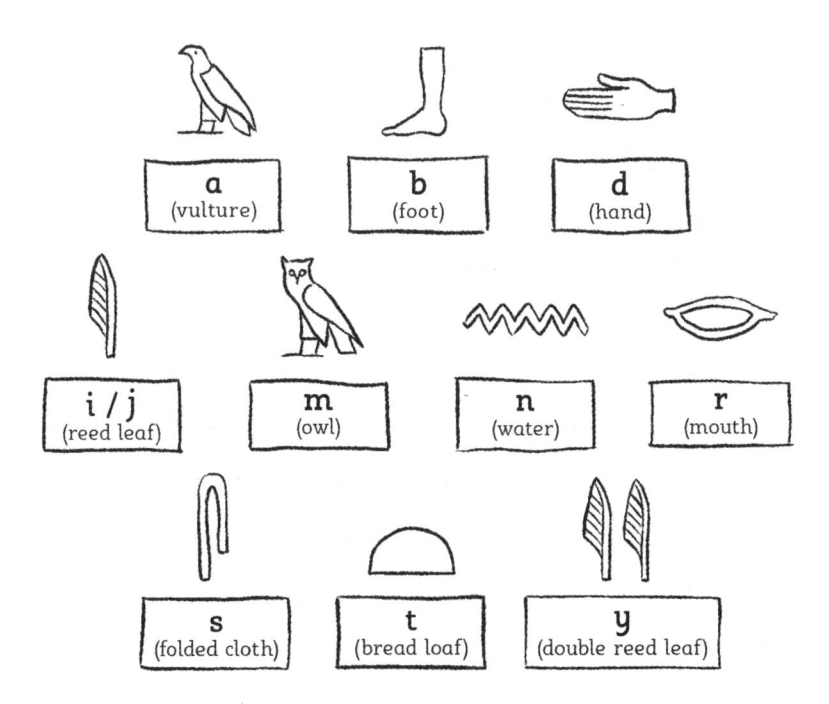

a (vulture)	b (foot)	d (hand)

i / j (reed leaf)	m (owl)	n (water)	r (mouth)

s (folded cloth)	t (bread loaf)	y (double reed leaf)

Knowing the meaning of the hieroglyphics on the rock enabled historians to read hundreds of other examples of hieroglyphics that had been discovered by archaeologists.

Often these were found on surviving fragments of papyrus paper or on the walls of ruined temples and tombs. These translations have slowly helped us to understand what life was like in ancient Egypt.

While women weren't normally allowed to train as scribes, many of them worked in the local temples as musicians and singers. These were important jobs too because the gods were often worshipped using music during religious festivals.

Some of their instruments were fairly basic, such as drums, cymbals, bells, and rattles called *sistrums*. Other instruments needed much more skill to play well. These included stringed instruments that were plucked like a guitar or played with a bow like a modern violin. Instruments played by blowing through a reed were also popular, like today's oboe or trumpet.

We know what these instruments looked like because silver trumpets and sistrums have been found by archaeologists and are now on display in museums.

Other instruments were included in wall paintings called murals. These show musicians playing the instruments on their own and also in groups. One even includes a cheironomist, which is a kind of conductor who may have been in charge of a whole orchestra.

The fact that musicians and singers are pictured in these paintings tells us how important music must have been to the Egyptians. We have no way of knowing what their music sounded like, and none of it was written down, but we do know the words to a few ancient Egyptian songs.

Not all of the songs were religious. One of them was something farmers used to sing while working under the sweltering sun. They may have sung the song to ask the gods to give them a good harvest or as a way to distract the farmworkers from their stiff backs and sore hands.

Talented musicians were respected by the Egyptians, so the women working in temples were often asked to play at non-religious events such as military parades and banquets for the very rich.

These banquets included dancing, which was also very popular. The guests never danced themselves, but professional dancers were paid to entertain them by dancing to the music.

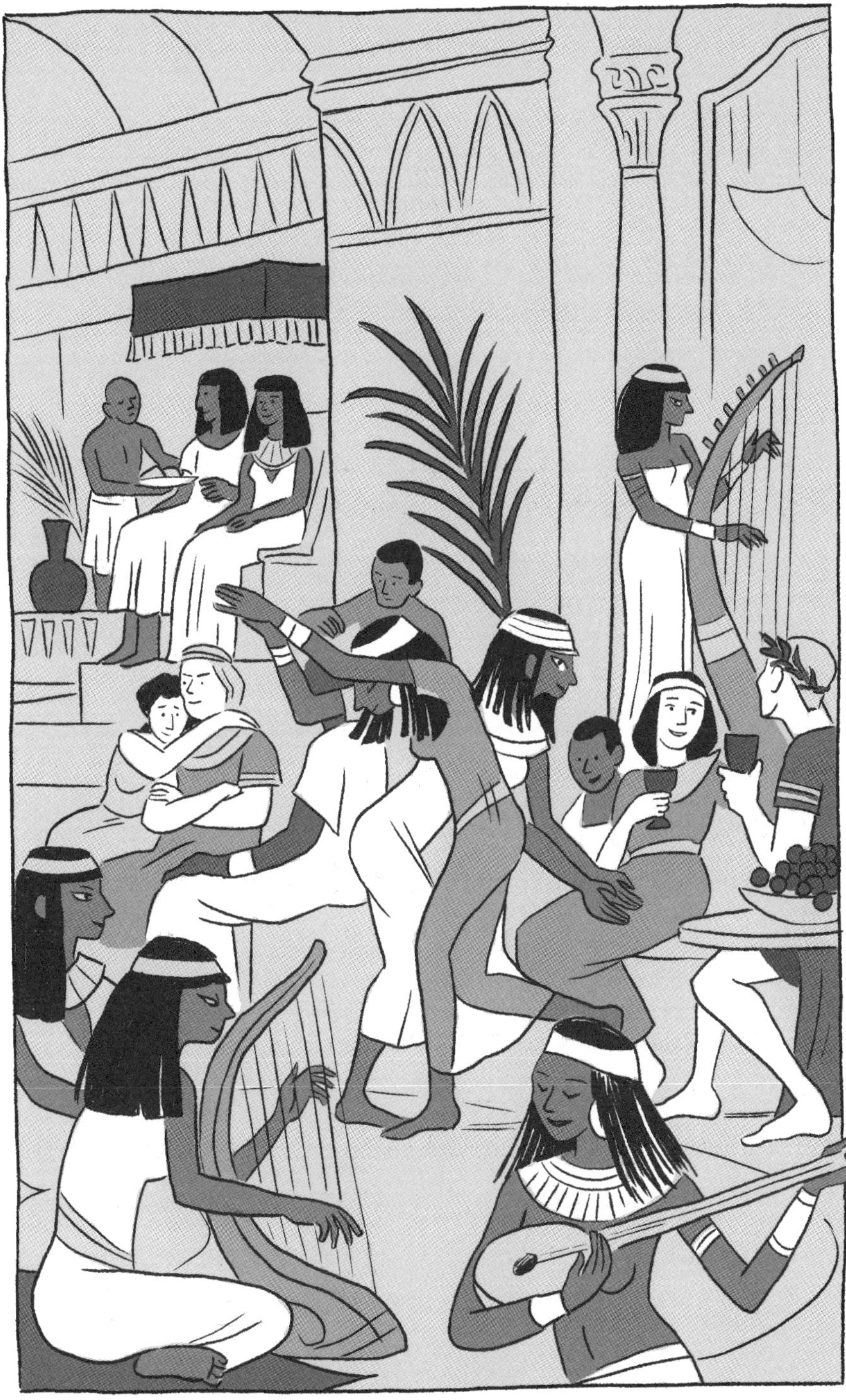

7
THE AFTERLIFE

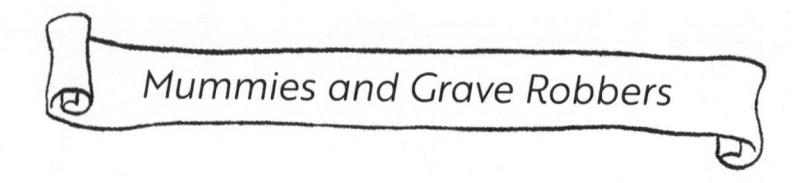

Mummies and Grave Robbers

The Egyptians believed that at the end of their normal lives they would go to the afterlife. Mummification was a vital part of this belief – a long, slow process to ensure that the dead person's body could pass safely over instead of just rotting away under the ground.

When we see a mummy in a museum, the first thing we're likely to notice is that it's been wrapped from head to toe in strips of linen cloth a bit like a long bandage. However, mummification involves much more than this, and each body had to undergo many weeks of careful preparation before being wrapped up in the cloth.

Mummification usually happened in a tent called an *ibu*. A priest and his assistants first washed the body using water from the River Nile and special wine.

It was then cut open so the lungs and other organs could be taken out. These were covered in a kind of natural salt called natron, which was found in the desert. The Egyptians used it to dry out the organs so they wouldn't go mouldy.

Strangely, the heart was left inside the body because Egyptians believed it contained a person's memories and their intelligence. However, the brain was always removed, by sticking a long metal hook up the person's nose and pulling it out.

Natron was also packed inside the body to dry it. This would take 40 days and then it could be washed again and rubbed with rich-smelling oils.

The Mummification Process

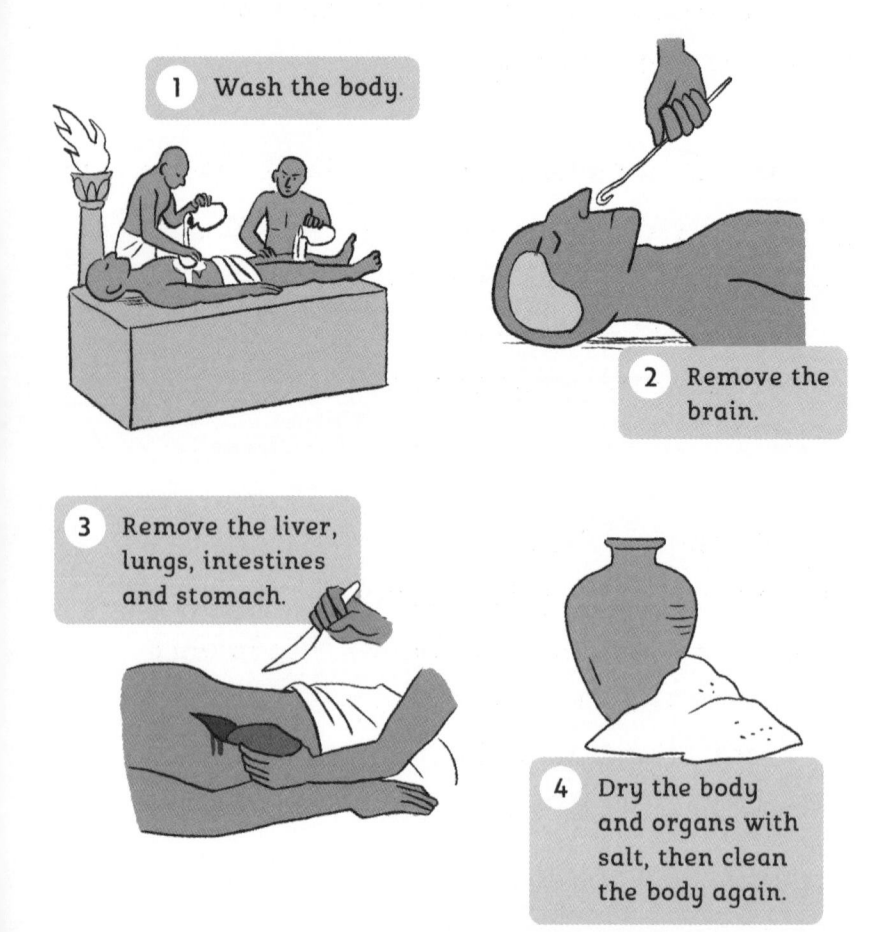

1. Wash the body.

2. Remove the brain.

3. Remove the liver, lungs, intestines and stomach.

4. Dry the body and organs with salt, then clean the body again.

THE AFTERLIFE

The organs were wrapped in linen and stored in four small stone or pottery containers called canopic jars. The lids of the jars featured the animal heads of gods

5. Put the organs in the canopic jars.

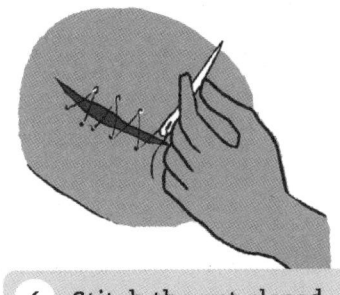

6. Stitch the cut closed.

7. Wrap the body in cloth strips.

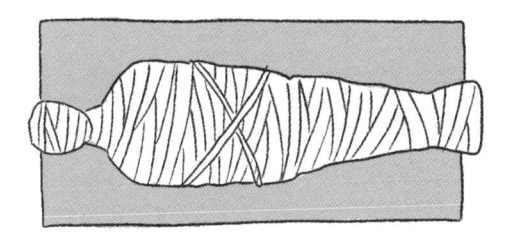

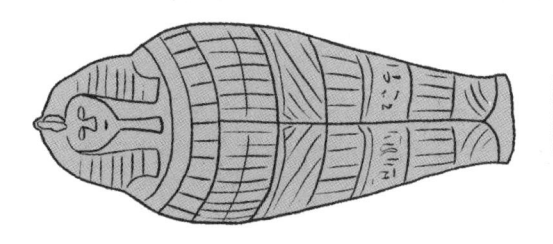

8. Place the body in the coffin.

THE AFTERLIFE

the Egyptians associated with mummification and death.

Wrapping even a small mummy needed around 150 metres of cloth, which was then painted with beeswax and resin. Resin is the sticky juice of a pine tree, and it was meant to protect the mummy by stiffening the cloth.

Tiny magic charms were often hidden between the cloth strips, and priests said special prayers and spells as the body was placed into a decorated coffin called a sarcophagus.

The sarcophagus and canopic jars were always buried together, but the tombs of rich Egyptians contained hundreds of other items.

The dead were believed to need everything in the afterlife that they used in real life, so Egyptian tombs were stuffed with furniture, clothes, games, fine jewellery, pots, plates,

THE AFTERLIFE 73

weapons, flowers and even food. The most amazing example of this is the tomb of Pharaoh Khufu, which included an entire ship more than 43 metres long.

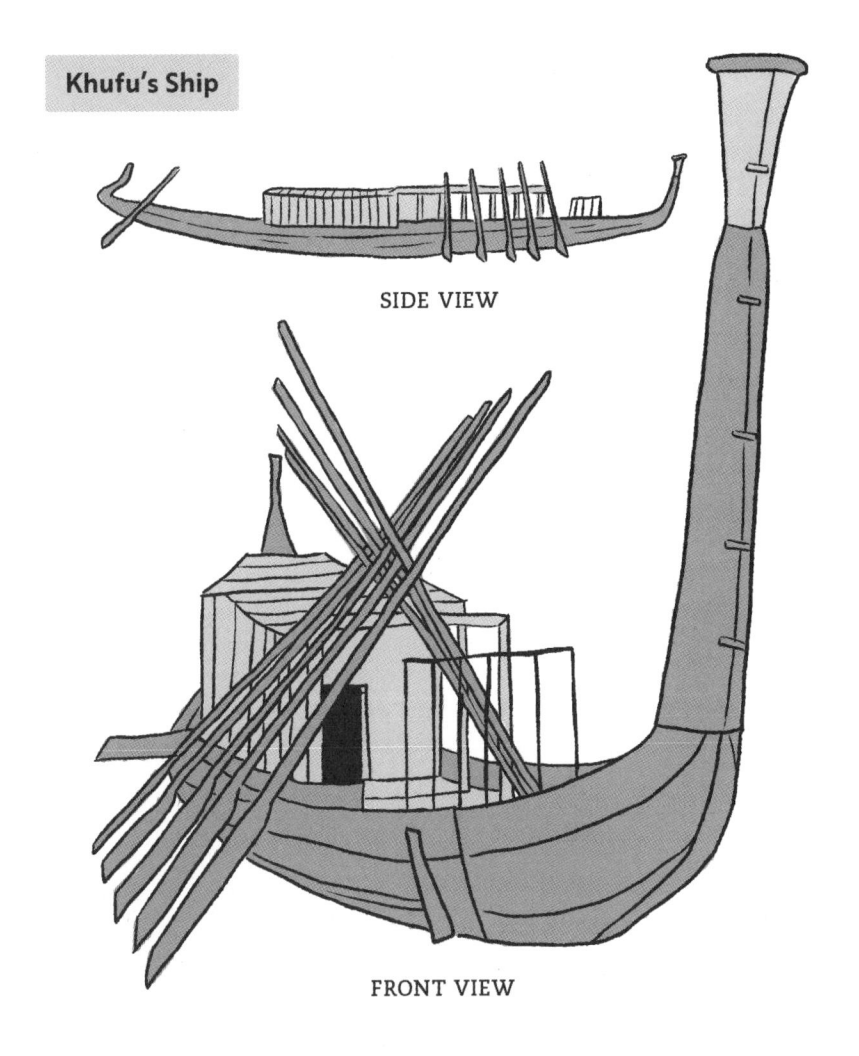

Khufu's Ship

SIDE VIEW

FRONT VIEW

Archaeologists call these things "grave goods". Unfortunately, because so many of them were rare and valuable, the tombs were often broken into.

Robbing a person's tomb was a very serious crime, and Egyptians hated the people who did it. Thieves who got caught were tortured and even put to death, but this didn't stop others doing it.

The pyramid builders tried all sorts of tricks to prevent the tombs of the pharaohs and their queens from being robbed.

For example, the entrance to a pyramid was always hidden behind a heavy stone block, and pyramids were built with different fake entrances to fool the robbers.

Inside the largest tombs were hundreds of metres of tunnels to confuse the robbers further. Some tunnels went up to secret

THE AFTERLIFE

chambers or rooms deep within the pyramid, and others went down underneath it.

It must have been easy for robbers to lose their way while crawling around in the dark, especially as some tunnels didn't lead anywhere.

Also, many of the real tunnels were filled in with rocks and other rubble after the pharaoh's burial to stop anyone getting in. Even if the rubble could be removed, most tunnels sloped steeply and were so narrow that it must have been hard for the robbers to remove anything valuable that they found inside.

But the tomb robbers succeeded despite all these measures to stop them.

Shockingly, some of the robbers were probably the same priests and officials who attended the burials. They knew exactly where to find the treasures. Others knew how to get in because they had helped build the pyramid in the first place.

The most energetic robbers worked in gangs to dig their own tunnels to the main burial chambers. This must have taken weeks of hard labour, but it may have been worth it if there was enough inside the pyramid for a gang to steal.

Thieves like these had no interest in the mummies but only stole the more precious items, including jewellery and other valuable metal objects. These were things they could easily sell, and some of the tomb robbers must have become very rich.

Almost every tomb was broken into, and eventually the Egyptians had to accept that pyramids offered no protection to a pharaoh and their possessions.

THE AFTERLIFE

They needed to try something else, and they decided to do it in a place called the Valley of the Kings.

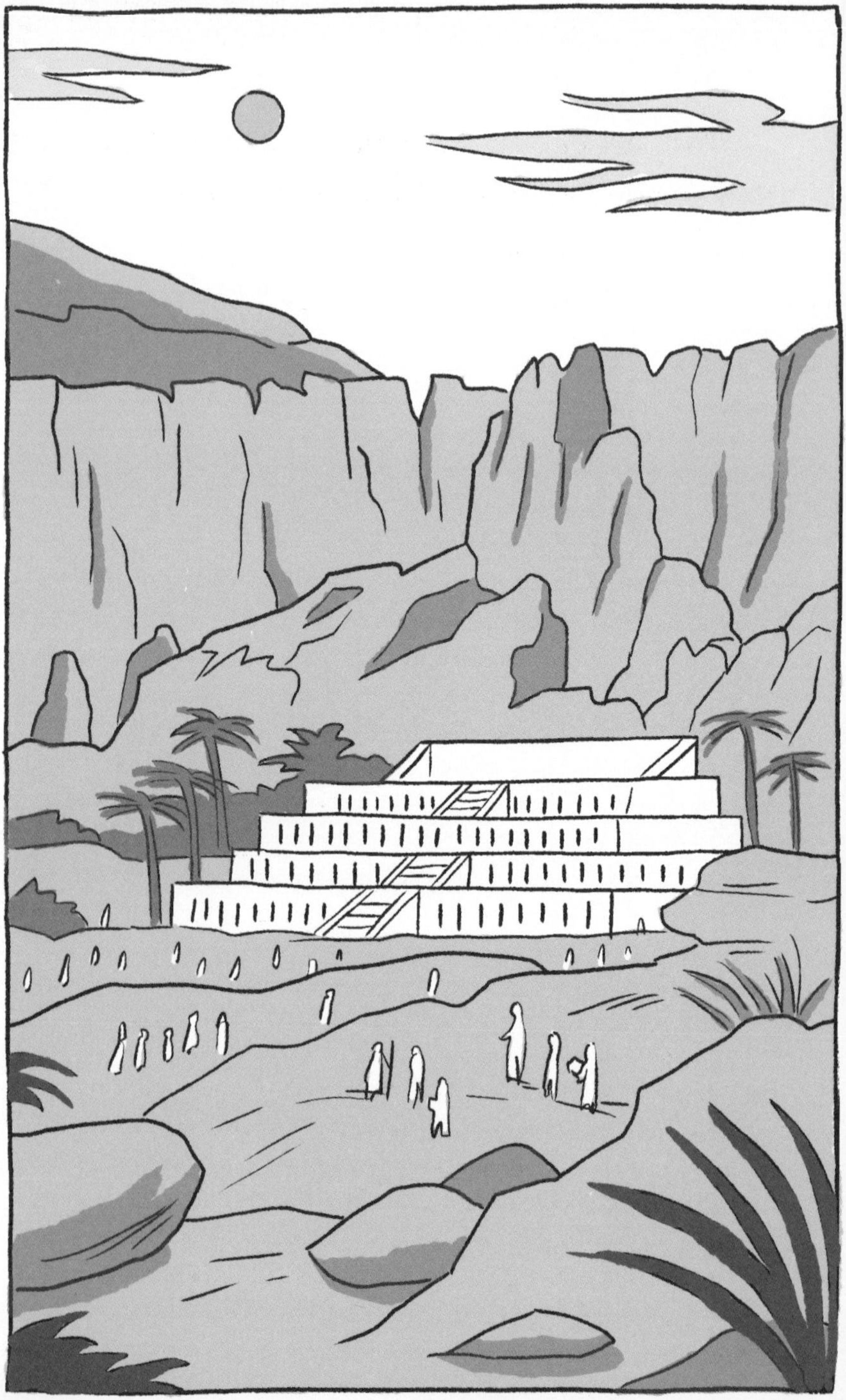

8
WONDERFUL THINGS

Tutankhamun and His Treasure

The Valley of the Kings was a vast area of rocky desert outside Thebes, the capital city of ancient Egypt. This area was remote and uninhabited, and seemed like a perfect hiding place away from the gangs of robbers.

The Egyptians didn't build enormous eye-catching tombs like the pyramids here, but secret underground tombs.

Most of these still had long entrance tunnels and many chambers for the possessions the dead would need in the afterlife. The public were forbidden to enter the Valley of the Kings, and the locations of the burials were never discussed in the hope that robbers wouldn't find them.

WONDERFUL THINGS

Unfortunately, this didn't work. More than 60 burials took place in the Valley of the Kings, but by the time archaeologists began exploring the area in the nineteenth century, all the tombs they found had already been robbed.

One archaeologist, named Howard Carter, believed he could find a royal tomb that hadn't been broken into. In the 1920s, he persuaded a rich Englishman called Lord Carnarvon to fund an expedition to look for it.

The pair were helped by dozens of Egyptian diggers and spent more than five years searching for the tomb of a young pharaoh called Tutankhamun.

Almost nothing was known about Tutankhamun in the 1920s. Many experts weren't sure he had ever existed and thought Carter was a bit crazy. Even Lord Carnarvon began to wonder if they would find anything valuable before he ran out of money.

By 1922, he had spent a fortune on the expedition, so he told Carter to stop digging. However, Carter begged for just one more chance, and Lord Carnarvon agreed.

In the autumn of 1922, Carter reported that he still hadn't found much, but on 4th November he had an amazing stroke of luck.

A young Egyptian boy tripped on a rock while bringing drinking water for the helpers searching for the tomb. When the boy looked down, he saw the rock was a piece of carved stone, so he showed it to the rest of the team.

Excitedly, the Egyptians began digging until they had uncovered a long flight of old stone steps. At the bottom, Carter found what looked like an ancient doorway. It showed a carving of nine enslaved people and Anubis, the jackal-headed god who was said to accompany the dead on their journey to the afterlife.

WONDERFUL THINGS 83

Carter was desperate to break down the door but knew he should tell Lord Carnarvon first, who was back in England. Lord Carnarvon left for Egypt immediately, but in the 1920s the journey took about two weeks. Lord Carnarvon was as keen as Carter to see what was behind the door, and he raced to Egypt by train, ship, another train and then on a donkey across the desert.

The carving of Anubis and the slaves was called a seal. The fact the door wasn't broken suggested that the tomb hadn't been robbed like all the others. Maybe Carter hadn't been wasting his time and a million pounds of Lord Carnarvon's money.

When they broke down the door, all they found was a long tunnel full of rubble. This took hours to clear, but at the end of it they could see another secret door.

Carter's hands shook with excitement as he made a small hole in the door and stuck in a lighted candle. Lord Carnarvon asked him what he could see, and Carter replied, "Wonderful things."

They soon realised that this was a royal tomb and that the mummy inside it was Tutankhamun. News of their discovery spread around the world, and Tutankhamun went from being unknown to the most famous pharaoh of all time. Even now, more than a hundred years later, it is still regarded by many experts as the greatest discovery in the history of archaeology.

Tutankhamun's worldwide fame can be seen as surprising because he didn't rule Egypt for very long and he was only a teenager when he died. He wasn't responsible for any famous buildings or monuments, or for conquering any of Egypt's enemies. Historians aren't even completely sure who his parents were or when he was born and how he died.

But he wasn't only famous because his tomb was the first (and only) pharaoh's tomb that had been found intact. It was also because the ancient items Carter and Lord Carnarvon discovered inside were so numerous and included some of the most fabulous treasures ever pulled from the ground.

WONDERFUL THINGS

Tutankhamun's tomb is actually one of the smallest in the whole Valley of the Kings, but it contained an astonishing 5,000 different objects in addition to the pharaoh's mummy.

Many items were simple everyday things, like bowls, shoes, and pots for olive oil, wine and food.

But others were far more spectacular, such as Tutankhamun's solid gold death mask, which is decorated with precious blue lapis lazuli. They also found his golden bed and golden throne, and a sparkling red stone sarcophagus.

These finds were so amazing and so numerous that historians are still busy examining them more than a century later.

This means we're still learning about the civilisation that produced them – and only beginning to understand the life and times of the young man who lay hidden beneath the desert sands.

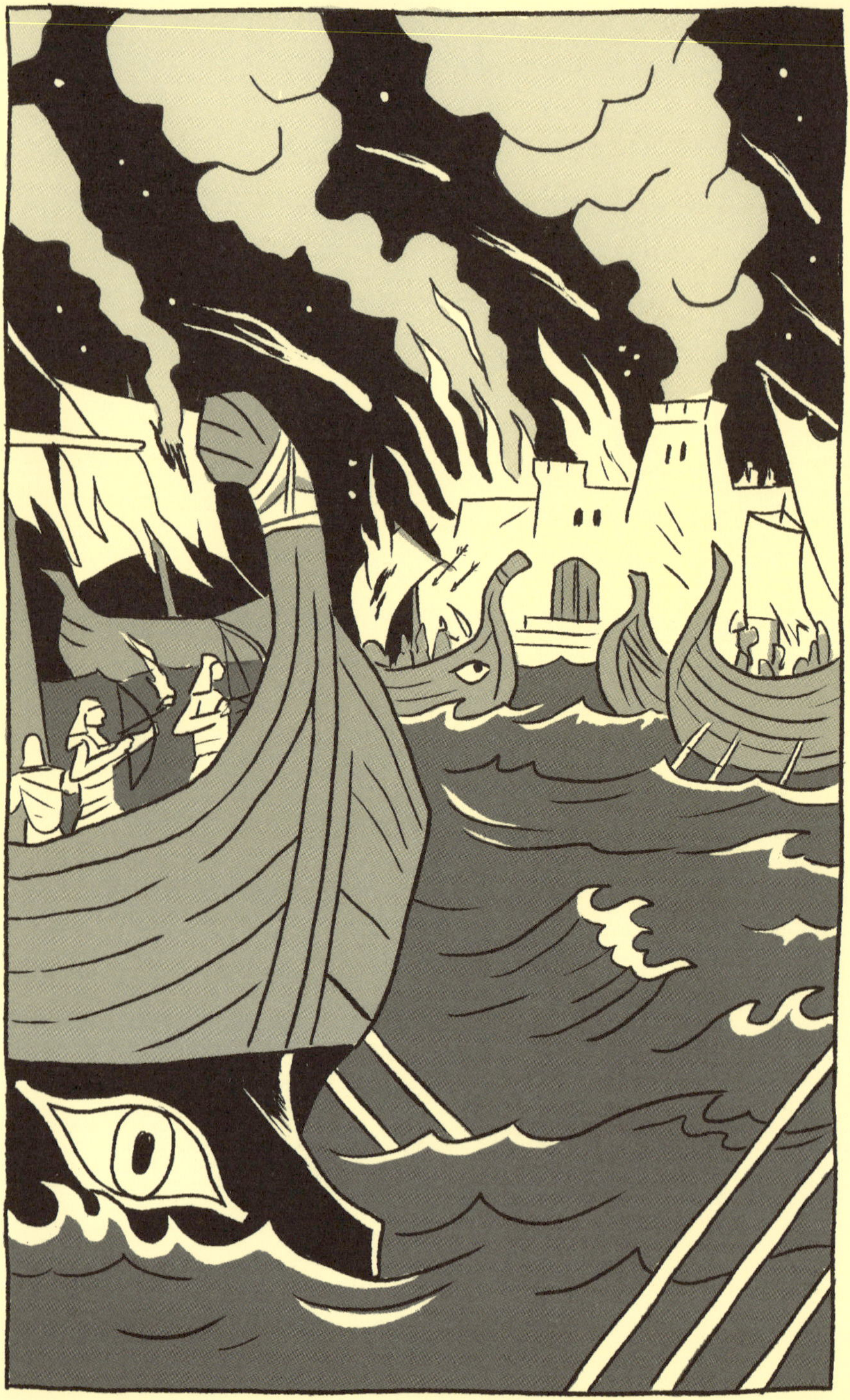

9
THE END OF THE EMPIRE

Egypt Today

Egypt still exists, and millions of Egyptians still rely on the River Nile for water, food and transport. However, their ancient empire is long gone.

It was invaded by a Persian army in 525 BCE and then by a famous Greek ruler called Alexander the Great. Eventually, the Romans took control of it in 30 BCE, a few months after defeating the Egyptian fleet at the Battle of Actium.

THE END OF THE EMPIRE

Many people believe that the last pharaoh, Cleopatra, killed herself by allowing a poisonous snake to sink its fangs into her.

Every year, increasing numbers of archaeologists join the hunt for clues to this incredible civilisation. Meanwhile, tourists flock to Egypt to learn more about the pharaohs, the people, their buildings and their gods. Nothing has been found to rival the treasures of Tutankhamun yet, but Cairo's new Grand Egyptian Museum shows that interest in the ancient Egyptians has never been greater.

Our books are tested
for children and young people by
children and young people.

Thanks to everyone who consulted on
a manuscript for their time and effort in
helping us to make our books better
for our readers.